# SUSPENSE STORIES V5

GREAT SUSPENSE STORIES



ABDUL RAHIM KHURRAM

# Contents

CHAPTER ONE

# Natalie Ayala

Natalie Ayala peered out the cab window as it slowly travelled down Hemmings Street, seeking for the familiar Sugar Maple in the backyard of the duplex she and her closest friend Miri owned. It had been little more than a year since her previous visit. It had been six years since she had resided there.

"I've arrived." She took a deep breath as the cab came to a halt in front of her home.

Natalie ran to the door, slinging her rucksack over her shoulder and checking the time on her phone. "3:27... I'm curious as to whether Miri is waiting for me."

She struggled for a while with the keys before opening the door.

"Door is open... And keep the lights on." She slung her suitcase onto a nearby chair and closed the door.

"Welcome home, my friend." Natalie giggled as she took in her surroundings.

"It's time for some tea." As she rounded the corner into the kitchen, she heard footsteps down the hall.

"I apologise, Mimi; I did not want to awaken you. I was just about to grab a cup of tea; would you want some?" Natalie peered over her shoulder and saw... A young guy in his twenties...

"Oh. I was unaware Mimi had company." Natalie flushed slightly at seeing the guy was dressed in boxers and a hurriedly thrown-on robe. "Are you dating Mimi?" She did not inform me that she obtained one."

"How did you get here? How did you get access to this place?" The guy inquired, concerned. "And who is this Mimi you keep mentioning?"

"My name is Natalie Ayala, and I gained access using my key." She propped it up. "'Mimi' is how I refer to Miri, my closest friend, roommate, and the young lady who lives here. Are you sure you couldn't figure it out?"

"Miri.... Which Miri Dragavei, maiden name Stafford, are you referring to?" The gentleman inquired.

"What was your maiden name?" Natalie arched her brow. "You mean she married someone else without informing me!?!? What the hell!?!? You're kidding, aren't you?"

"Yes, she married, and if you were truly her greatest friend, she would have informed you."

"You would believe that, wouldn't you?" Natalie shook her head in disbelief. "Wait.... Does it imply you're married to her?"

"No," she said, "Miri was my stepmother."

"What!?!? Certainly not! You seem to be in your mid-twenties!"

"I'm twenty-six years old, and I see nothing wrong with it. The funny thing is that you may be Miri's 'best friend' despite the fact that you seem to be younger than me!"

"No. What's weird is that, despite the fact that you're clearly older than Mimi, you-"

"Older!?!?" His gaze drew inward. "Are you delusory? You claim to be Miri's closest friend, yet you have no idea how old she would be today!"

"What are you referring to?" I am quite aware of Mimi's age! You are the one who is ignorant!" Natalie attempted to shove her way past him.

"How far do you believe you're going?" The guy extended his arm in an attempt to dissuade her.

"I'm going to track down Mimi and see why this insane dude is in my home!"

"You must go. Now!" He took her arm in his grip.

"Refrain from touching me!" I have no clue who you are or why you are in my home, but if you do not leave immediately, I will contact the authorities!" Natalie sprang from of his grasp and clutched her phone.

"Wait a minute. There is no need to contact the authorities." A second gentleman entered the room. "Permit me to begin by introducing myself. Mark Dragavei is my name, and here is my kid Norma."

"Perfect, now I can identify the mysterious guys that broke into my home without permission." Natalie let out a snarl.

"I apologise, Dad; I didn't intend to wake you." Norma expressed regret. "However, that was not my fault." He locked his gaze on Natalie. "However, now that you're standing, you may order this female to go. I believe she is under the influence of something. She continues to speak as if she owns the house, referring to Miri as her closest friend, and other such nonsense."

"As odd as this may seem, she may be speaking the truth." Mr. Dragavei gently squeezed his son's shoulder. "Please let me to handle this." He took a stride toward Natalie, who took a step away from him.

"Another step closer, and I'm going to call the cops." I really mean it." Natalie put her phone up for the guys to check the screen. 911 was dialled, her thumb trembling over the call button.

Mr. Dragavei paused before extracting his own phone. "This is Miri and you." That was never a question.

On the phone, there was a photograph of two young ladies. Natalie with a short, untidy pixie cut. Miri, on the other hand, wore her long wavy blonde hair back in a braid that draped over her shoulder. Both girls were appropriately attired for exploration in the wild outdoors.

Natalie cast a glimpse at Mark's phone and sighed. "That is correct. We shot the photograph last summer on our vacation." She took a step back and lowered her own phone. "However, why do you own it?"

"Your given name is Natalie Ayala." Once again, this is not a question.

"You did not respond to my inquiry."

"Because I am Miri's spouse," he said. Or... at the very least, I was." Mr. Dragavei's eyes widened slightly.

“Meaning?”

"I‘m not quite certain what's happening on... nonetheless, I will make every effort to clarify." He made a move toward the sofa. "Please have a seat. Norma will brew some tea for everyone." And he took a seat himself.

Norma nodded and entered the kitchen, while Natalie reclined on her unique recliner, which seemed strangely antique....

Mr. Dragavei talked in hushed tones. "Would you kindly listen to what I have to say without interfering?" You and Miri graduated from high school in fourteen and purchased this half of the duplex jointly, correct?"

Natalie gave a nod.

“Good.” He persisted. "You received a scholarship and attended college in another nation, whereas Miri has just recently entered the workforce. You'd pay each other a visit each year and spend the summer together. By twenty-twenty, you had completed your studies and were preparing to return. However, the aircraft on which you were travelling vanished and-"

"Stop! What do you mean when you say it'disappeared'? My aircraft was unharmed. It was not even close to being late." Natalie was adamant.

"I believe I requested that you refrain from interfering."

"Sorry."

"I met Miri in March of twenty-twenty. We collaborated. You were due to return in October of the same year, but as I already said, your aircraft vanished. Nobody has ever discovered any signs of it. Miri was distraught. It took five years before she said that she had accepted the fact that you would not return, but I'm not sure she ever really did. We married the next year. Norma is a descendant of my first marriage. It wasn't very long, and sadly, neither was my second."

"Do you honestly suppose I'm going to believe this?" Natalie inquired suspiciously.

"Not quite, but it is true."

"Indeed it is." Her eyes rolled.

"Your phone should synchronise automatically with the satellites, correct?"

"Indeed."

"Confirm the date."

Natalie retrieved her phone and examined the date for the first time since boarding the aircraft. October 27, it said. The day she was scheduled to come... wait a minute... the year is 2037... Her head jolted forward. "I refuse to believe this! This is a ruse! You've got to be hacking my phone... or something..."

"I made no changes to your phone. It is, in fact, twenty-seven."

"However, it is im-impossible..." Natalie was taken aback. This could not possibly be true. Right?

"Unfortunately, I'm going to have to break some more awful news to you. Miri passed away in the year twenty-seven. Exactly ten years ago."

This was not the case. This cannot be true. Mimi is no longer alive. 2037. This was a figment of my imagination. That was unavoidable. That was the only logical conclusion... She remained on the aircraft. She would awaken at any minute now. It would be 2020, and the moment she switched on her phone, she would get a call from Mimi, who would be waiting outside to take her home. That is correct; this whole experience was a dream. Natalie clenched her eyes. She would soon reawaken. However, she did not.

After two hours, twelve cups of tea, an equal number of visits to the restroom, and five frantic outbursts, Natalie was soothed, more out of tiredness than comprehension of the issue. She reclined on the sofa, expressionless, looking up at the ceiling.

"So allow me to set the record straight." Norma was likewise having difficulty comprehending. "Seventeen years ago, she was Miri's closest friend, who vanished. And for some reason, she's still twenty-four years old, despite the fact that she should be fifteen years my senior."

"I'm not sure I understand it either, but it seems to be the case." Mr. Dragavei shook his head in disbelief.

"If... I am indeed from the past... or any other nonsense... therefore everyone else on the aircraft is as well... correct? Wouldn't it elicit widespread terror or something..." Natalie muttered barely loud enough to be heard above a whisper, her arms concealing her face.

"She is correct!" Norma sprang to his feet and switched on the television to the local news channel.

"-passenger aircraft disappeared above the Bermuda Triangle. Exactly seventeen years later, at 12:45 a.m., the identical airliner landed at Los Angeles International Airport. Simultaneously, it was scheduled to return in 2020. According to others, the aircraft may have gone through a wormhole and into the future. Others have postulated extraterrestrials. However, nothing can be confirmed at the moment. Government authorities and medical specialists are presently attempting to locate all passengers in order to collect information and ensure that no one suffers any major medical consequences." The news anchorman said exaggeratedly. "We will keep you updated when new information becomes available. For KYI-57, this is David Smith."

Norma turned off the television as adverts began to play. "Are you saying you passed through a wormhole?" Interesting..."

"This is just guesswork." Mark muttered something.

"How... did it... occur?" Natalie took a breath.

"Were you not paying attention? Nobody is certain how the aircraft entered the future." Norma shook his head in disbelief.

"That is not the case..... That is, with Mimi..." Natalie turned onto her side and locked her gaze on Norma. "How did she pass away?"

"'That." He brushed his hair back and gazed at his father. "Dad?"

Mr. Dragavei exhaled a sigh. "Following the plane's disappearance, Miri started researching folklore, news stories, documentaries, and whatever other material she could obtain. Initially, she was able to manage her schedule rather well, but she developed an obsession. She would spend days without eating or drinking. It became so severe that she was hospitalised. Following that, she calmed down and said that coming so near to death made her realise she didn't want to squander her life on a fruitless pursuit.

"She improved, or at least improved somewhat. She fell into a deep depression for a while thereafter, but she maintained her composure and even accepted my proposal. I assumed she would eventually get over you, but I was mistaken. I eventually discovered that she never stopped seeking, analysing, and researching whatever she came across that had to do with the Bermuda Triangle or missing aircraft." Mark took another drink of his tea and sighed.

"In July of twenty-seven, Miri announced that she was going on a vacation with a group of her pals. I believed it would benefit her, and hence did not question it. I discovered a month later that she had really gone on some arranged adventure. A storm hit, and the ship they were using sank. That ship carried thirty-eight passengers. There was only one survivor." Mr. Dragavei raised his eyes to his phone and arose. "I have to go to work in a few hours, so I'm going to attempt to catch up on sleep." And he departed.

It took many minutes for him to speak again.

"So Mimi's death is all my responsibility." Natalie's voice was deafeningly silent.

"I realise this is an inopportune moment to say this, but... welcome home." Norma wanted to console Natalie but lacked the necessary skills.

Natalie cast a bemused glance around the room. "Yeah. Indeed, welcome home."

CHAPTER TWO

# Never touch what's not yours

Many times, we may wonder what is blowing in the woods, or how the wind blows, and it may be a frightening experience. All I can remember is a very cold and brisk night when I was going home from choir practise on my alone. I accidentally bumped into a stranger, and I know the person was aware of the collision, but the individual was unable to see or hear me. Like the wind, I could hear and see the person talking and moving about around. This individual seemed to have resurrected from the dead and was really frightening. His clothing were tattered and shredded, and he was missing an arm on the left side. As a result, I'm terrified to inquire as to what transpired since the voice of this individual seemed like thunder clapping from a terrifying thunderstorm. It was as if the guy evaporated into thin air as I proceeded on my journcy back home. So I took a deep breath and was so relieved that I sprinted back home. I attempted to contact my closest buddy to tell her what had occurred, but her phone was always busy. All of the lights in my home began to flicker on and off, and I recognised the voice of the person who had spoken to me earlier. Suddenly, the lights in my home began to flash as he went about the room. I was hyperventilating since I'd never seen anything like this before and it was completely unexpected. He began to mutter things that I was unable to comprehend, and there was no way for me to communicate with him since he was unable to hear or see what I was saying. I remained still to see what would happen next, and he immediately started throwing my furniture all over the place and reaching out as if to grab me, but I managed to get away as quickly as I could. Following my fall, I observed blood dripping down the inside of my leg. The next thing I remember, I'm collapsing. The first thing I noticed when I awoke was my closest buddy calling to see how I was doing in the hospital. I burst into tears because I knew no one would believe that I had accidentally bumped into someone who could feel the bump but couldn't hear or see me. Despite the fact that I could see and hear this individual, I couldn't figure out what he was attempting to say or why he had chosen me. My closest buddy escorted me to the hospital, where the doctor informed me that I would need to remain overnight for observation. Even though I was terrified to remain, I made an effort not to show that I was afraid. There was this figure that arrived in my chamber, and it was pitch black, but he was radiating a dazzling light. He stated in that loud and booming voice, "I come for your soul," and I yelled, but no one could hear me because it was too late. So I continued relaying the storey, and then I broke down and sobbed because I believed I was dead. The individual vanishes again again, but this time a second person arrives who was also invisible but could hear and see me, and this person is likewise invisible. She inquired as to whether "Marcus" had been troubling you, and I was unable to respond since I was too terrified. She said that

"Marcus" ran into me today, but that he was unable to hear or see me. So I tried to remain cool and responded, "Yes, I think it was him," after a moment's thought. She confirmed that it was him, noting that he had been dead for 12 years and had been disturbing the living ever since. It was explained to me that "Marcus's" parents adopted him and educated him at some of the best schools in the area. One day, a gang of youths beat him to death and severed his limb from his body. For a few hours at the hospital, he maintained his conscientiousness. He informed his parents that he would be returning to murder everyone who had assaulted him that day. The reason he continues to harass you is because you are acquainted with the girl who dated one of the men who assisted in his murder. As soon as I started crying, she vanished as well. That leaves me with a dilemma. So I dialled my friend's phone number and attempted to explain everything to her, but she didn't pick up the phone. When I arrived at her residence, I discovered that she had committed suicide by her own hand. It looked that she had committed suicide, but I knew otherwise. "Marcus" is responsible for her death, and I might be next. What is it about stumbling into a deceased person that causes all of these issues for the living? This time it was the other person who could hear and see me who came up. She said that she is going to assist you since you are a victim of crime. She instructed me to call my friend's boyfriend and arrange a meeting with him. She was told that hc had the solution in his book bag, which she found to be true. It didn't make any sense, but I decided to give it a go anyhow. When I went to see my best friend's boyfriend, he was still grieving over her loss, so I left. So I told everything that had occurred, and he was delighted to assist me. And as a result, he dug inside his bookbag and yanked out an arm of "Marcus," the guy I had run into earlier today. I shouted so loudly that his cat screeched in response. The reason he was still carrying this person's arm in his backpack was because he had won the bet, I discovered when I questioned him about it. They were all in agreement that the individual should be beaten, but one of the members of the gang wanted him dead. That's correct, it's the boyfriend of one of my friends. As a result, he bet them that they would be unable to chop off his arm and store it in their bookbag for a year. He knew they wouldn't do it, and he proved them wrong, therefore he won the bet. During that period, he kept the arm in a glass case in his bookbag for safekeeping. I was terrified of it because, after witnessing what that guy was capable of, I was concerned that he may still try to murder me. So I asked my friend's boyfriend for an arm, and he agreed since the one-year anniversary of their relationship occurred today. It would also explain all of the unusual occurrences that have occurred in the lead-up to Halloween. The arm was restored, and the individual was allowed to return to his tomb in peace, vowing never to hurt another live soul again. As a moral to this tale, never steal anything that doesn't rightfully belong to you, and if you do, please return it immediately since lives may be at stake.

CHAPTER THREE

# Nonnie

I walked into the front door and locked it behind me, keeping the cold chill out. To go into the shower, I hurriedly opened the glass door and went into the shower while still fully clad in my clothes. The water had seeped through my clothing, and I had to undress down to my underwear. I went to the store and bought a bar of lavender-scented soap since I couldn't determine whether I should wash or burn the clothing I'd found. As I scraped my hands over the water, the water became a lovely, sudsy pink. I stood there and watched the gory run-off circle the drainage pipe.

My thoughts began to clarify as the water began to recede. As soon as I came down from my adrenaline high, I set about making a strategy. After my shower, I'd put my clothing in a bag and toss them in the trash. Trash collection would take place in the morning, and then they'd be gone for good. As soon as I was certain that every single trace of blood splatter had been removed from my body, I walked outside and dried off. I threw on my sweatpants and went to the office.

Using a garbage bag from the kitchen, I threw away my ruined garments and cleaned up the mess. I took a shower with bleach and tossed the cleaning items in the laundry basket with my clothing. The bag was tied in a triple knot and thrown into the dustbin once it was tied. I rolled the trash can out to the curb. After that, I went on with my life.

The television in my neighbor's living room was playing so loudly that I couldn't hear the soap opera I was attempting to watch while sitting in my own living room. It wasn't the first time the neighbor's television had intruded on my space, and it was unlikely to be the last. It was time to get dressed, so I put on a terrycloth bathrobe (since no self-respecting lady would walk outdoors in her pyjamas!) and slipped my feet into a pair of slippers. I went next door to Mrs. Sherny's house to urge her to turn it down. The same thing occurred every December, and it happened every time one of my soaps was on.

I went inside the building after ringing the bell once and inserting my key. Fortunately, Mrs. Sherny had provided me with a key so that I wouldn't have to get out of my chair. The doorbell was only a politeness on their behalf. Draped in her regular parrot-green house dress, Mrs. Sherny was comfortably ensconced into her easy chair. A ninety-seven year old lady with wispy purple hair, she was a sight to see. She had a pair of enormous, thick spectacles that made her eyes seem bulgy but didn't appear to do anything to improve her eyesight in any way.

"Your television volume is too loud once again," I said. Mrs. Sherny didn't say anything and just stared at me. I made a motion with my finger to the television and then to my ear. Mrs. Sherny remained silent during the conversation. I went in search of the remote. It was resting on top of a large-print Agatha Christie book that I had on the sofa table when I discovered it. I brought it up to my ear and punched the lower volume button with great force. "Does your hearing aid battery need to be recharged again?"

Mrs. Sherny remained deafeningly silent once again. She was wearing a hearing aid in her left ear, so I removed it and went to the kitchen drawer to get a new battery. I inserted the fresh battery into the gadget and then reinserted the little device into her ear. She didn't make a sound.

"I'm going to make banana bread later." The next day, I'll bring some over." On my way out, I shut her door behind me.

When I returned home, I immediately started working on the banana bread. There was no sense in watching daytime talk programmes anymore since my soaps were over. I looked in my refrigerator for eggs; I didn't want to go to the grocery store, but I would if I had to if I didn't have enough. I was relieved to see that I had a whole carton. I prepared my oven and began peeling bananas right away.

At the end of the day, I had three loaves of banana bread cooling on the kitchen counter. I showered and dressed in a professional manner. I covered one loaf of bread in plastic wrap after it had cooled down sufficiently. This time, instead of walking down the driveway to the pavement, I wore tennis shoes instead of slippers and cut across the yards.

Mrs. Sherny's driveway had a strange automobile parked in it, and she was suspicious. It was dark and glistening to an almost indecent degree. It took me a while to decide since I was concerned about disrupting her with guests. I walked over to see what was going on. Besides, I reasoned, having visitors would provide an excuse for me to get out of there as soon as possible. Whenever I spoke with Mrs. Sherny, the conversation was usually one-sided and uncomfortable. I went up to the door and rang it. It was opened relatively soon, which was unusual. A tall, well-dressed guy in a suit stood before me, his hand resting on a notebook.

"I'm on the lookout for Mrs. Sherny," I said. The banana bread I gave her was a gift from me.

"Can you tell me when was the last time you saw her?" While we were talking, the guy kept his gaze on me from side to side. I got the chills when I saw that.

"It was this morning," I responded.

"Did you bring her some banana bread this morning?" To be honest, I thought that was a strange question. Why would I bring her banana bread twice in the same day, you may wonder.

"No, I'm taking it with me right now. Every year at Christmas, I bring her some. That is, not on Christmas-Christmas, but rather on Christmas-Christmas, exactly as for Christmas. Christmas is celebrated on the 23rd, which does not have a formal name like Christmas."

"What's with the 23rd?" the guy inquired. I felt that was a little disrespectful. Who has a problem with someone giving a present in a certain way? Who was he to interrogate me in the first place?

I cook banana bread on that day. " "Does Mrs. Sherny happen to be here?" I attempted to peep inside the home from behind him.

"Oh, she's here, no problem. According to the medical examiner, the body had been in the same place for a decade."

"Do you mean medical examiner?" I went through it again.

"She's no longer alive. The body of a mummified man is in the living room. As a result, I think it pretty fascinating that you happened to see her earlier this morning."

"That can't possibly be the case. What sort of twisted joke is this, you may wonder. "And who exactly are you?"

This was insane, and I mean that in the most literal sense.

"Hello, my name is Detective Martin, and no one is kidding around here. You said that you send her banana bread on an annual basis. "Can you tell me how long this has been going on?"

Ten years would have passed this year. On the 23rd, I plan to bake banana bread. Three loaves of bread. Three of them were for me, one for my sister, and the third was for Mrs. Sherny. Then I bring it over here and put it on the kitchen counter for her."

"Doesn't it strike you as strange that she never eats the bread?"

She, of course, consumed the bread. I forced my way through the strange guy and inside the home. The only thing left for Mrs. Sherny was to convey to him that she was not dead and that she adored the banana bread. Mrs.desiccated Sherny's corpse, on the other hand, was pushed up in her chair.

The investigator pointed to the kitchen counter with his index finger. Nine loaves of rotten banana bread were on the counter, unopened and unattended. But it was the bloody message scribbled on the white blanket that covered Mrs. Sherny's lap that made me the most uncomfortable. It was simply one word:

Nonnie.

CHAPTER FOUR

# Peter Lopez

As I sat on the barber's chair made of red leather, I awaited the arrival of the cape.

I'd been in line for two hours with what seemed like every male in the city. As we waited for our turn at Peter's Cuts, we spoke among ourselves in various levels of scruffiness. Now that I was comfortably seated, the sensation of weightlessness in my feet was exhilarating.

On this particular day, John was in attendance. The guy in the chair next to me was having his head trimmed, and I closed my eyes and listened to his conversation while Peter sterilised his scissors.

Lopez was nothing more than an automaton. On that particular day, he'd opened at 7AM and pledged to remain open until he'd shaved the heads of every male in line. It was about 6 p.m., two hours beyond his usual closing time.

When the cape was snapped clear of hair, I heard a tap of steel on the sink, followed by a few test snips. After Peter finished cutting my hair, he spritzed me with a minty aftershave. Previously, he'd informed me that it was the same one his father used when this was his store.

Then he inquired, "Trim, Nathan?"

That's what I requested.

When he suddenly stopped moving, I could feel it just as clearly as I could hear him.

The sound of his belly laughing filled the store. When he said, "You're kidding, aren't you?" Shave it? What are you talking about?

Peter had spent years grooming my hair here in this chair, on several occasions every two weeks. A betrayal was sensed.

It began with a number one above my ears, transitioned into temple fuzz that was more salt than pepper, and finished with Peter's distinctive tapering V pointing down my neck. It was a beautiful haircut by any standard. Peter said that the golden ratio was used to determine the proportions of my haircut. The first time I had my hair trimmed by Peter, I vowed never to go anyplace else again.

Shave it, screamed my phoney bravery as I waited in line for hours for my turn at a hairdresser's chair.

This masterpiece? "he said with his hands in circles around my head. "Is this my best work?"

"Peter, I'm really sorry. As much as I appreciate your efforts, I have no idea when we'll be able to meet again."

Slowly, Peter frowned and moaned. That's why I'm here.

"I'm very sorry," I said.

"It's OK, Nathan. It's time for your eleventh haircut of the day.

"Is this virus making everyone crazy?"

To be fair to the shutdown, it's excellent for business this week. Man, I have no idea what I'm going to do.

Even though the virus hadn't yet reached our city, it was already taking lives. I took a glance at Peter in the mirror, and I was surprised. After years of carrying the weight of his family and responsibilities, he seemed frail and exhausted. Anxiety crept into my stomach as I considered my own children, who seemed blissfully ignorant of just how close we were to being stranded on the street. My supervisor would ring at any time to inform me that my contract had been suspended until further notice. A little savings account and my parents‘ beach house on the coast were options if we could not pay our rent, but who would assist us in moving out if it became necessary?

Small cash-only enterprises like Peter' Cuts were likely to be crippled by the proclamation of enforced quarantine for all citizens. At the very least, he was able to cash in on his efforts today. Even at a price of $30 per person, the queue had to have gone around the block.

Peter put the scissors aside and turned on the clippers with a sigh of resignation. "What's the second?"

I said, "Let's go with the one," that we take a chance. "At the very least, it gives me a week."

When Peter lifted his brows to modify the shape, it was clear that he was thinking clearly.

My pulse rate accelerated as the buzzing of the clippers filled my ears. I felt as if I were going to be given the deadly injection.

What's wrong?" Peter made the comment.

I drew in a big breath. I'd prepared myself for this. Hope, not reality, prompted me to say "It will grow back," rather than the truth.

Peter was moving the clippers from my forehead to my neck in a series of rows. A farmer gathers grey wheat for the threshing floor. The tufts of hair on my head began to fall out as I observed them with a macabre interest. Some of my hair was once such a part of me that when it came out, I was shocked it didn't hurt. It was good to have the hair from the back of my neck touch my face, while the hairs from the front rested on my lap. Stacks of silver nests stacked up on the cape under my palms. I loosened my grasp and let my fingers to regain their blood supply.

The mounting anxiety I was feeling as I saw the loss of my cherished hair was released when I blew air into my face. I was considering making a joke about leaving my head half-shaved, but the line outside was growing more impatient.

There was a noticeable rise in the intensity of the men's patient murmurs as they waited for their turn.

Man: "Hello! I'm looking for you!" It's my time, asshole, wait my turn!

My attention was drawn to some scuffle at the front entrance by Peter, who had his clippers firmly in hand despite the fact that a slip would have made little difference to the outcome.

An greasy hoodie-clad young guy was puffing at the entrance. As the news got more and more worrisome, the despair in his eyes became more and clearer to us all. We'd seen it on the news: desperate people taking over towns and nations. It was the face of pain we'd told ourselves not to judge harshly since, ultimately, it was inevitable that we'd experience it too, as shown in numerous zombie apocalypse movies.

After yet another futile trip to the supermarket, my neighbour told me, "Don't cast aspersions on these poor people." "We don't know what's going on in their personal life." Just trying to make ends meet for the people they love."

Despite my rage at the selfishness of these paranoid prepping devils, I agreed in public.

Despite his heavy breathing, the stranger remained motionless at the doorway of Peter's home and did not move. This guy was being attacked by the mob behind him as they all tried to rush through the entrance at the same time, allowing none of them to get through. His hands were held aloft in a peace gesture as he approached the guy. His response was, "Easy, buddy."

Disdainful and even pitying, the man's gaze fell on him as if being a barber were a horrible occupation for a redhead.

"Sir, may I assist you?" Peter spoke confidently.

The guy continued to huff and puff as John cautiously closed the door on the boiling mob on the street behind him.

"Sir, do you need to get a haircut?" Peter made the comment.

He took a big gulp. As he muttered, "Fuck your haircut, dude," his voice sounded like a whisper.

Peter encouraged calm before John the Irishman, whose blood was renowned for its rapidity, could stab the guy with his scissors. "Jim, it's nothing."

Even though John was in control of the situation up to this point, Peter's response to John's urging to put the pistol down changed my mind.

During this time, I saw the man's hoodie concealing a black revolver that was just visible in his pocket. The hold on the weapon had worn down his fingers to a pale whiteness.

The guy responded, "There's nothing to work out, mate." "You survive another day if you give me the money in your till there."

Even though it was against my better judgement, I made a sound that I mistakenly believed to be encouraging remarks. Something to bring the issue under control. "Whoah," all I could manage to say out of sheer adrenaline and disbelief at what was happening.

Man, what the fuck are you calling me?' The shooter yelled as he drew his revolver and aimed it at me. It trembled in his cadaverous paw.

"None of that," I said. The narrator says, "I just want us all to settle down."

"I feel at ease. And when this motherfucker emptied his till, I'll be a lot calmer." A gun was slung in Peter's direction.

Peter said, "Alright, okay."

He seemed to be a typical holdup victim, sweating through his white shirt and raising his arms in surrender. Because it seemed to be too corny to be genuine, I half-expected a director to yell, "Cut!"

As they detailed the issue to—who?—the police?—the men outside were ranting and gesticulating violently into their phones. What are the chances of getting a girlfriend now? Who would have thought it possible these days. Some of the people in the room were recording, and it made me feel bad about spending thirty dollars on a haircut that I could have had done for free with the help of my beard trimmer by the people who weren't chatting on their phones.

Man behind the register called out for Peter, "Open it," as he backed him up to where he was.

Peter dropped his hands to the register and murmured, "OK, friend." "Take a deep breath."

The man's eyes were closed for a brief while as if he were attempting to recall something. If one of you tells me to calm down again, I'll kill you both, do you understand?" he said with the barrel of his pistol slapped on his forehead.

As Peter responded, "OK, I'll do that." "We've got everything under control."

I'd have assumed Peter had done it more than once if I hadn't known better. His hands remained steady as they dipped toward the register's buttons, lowering one at a time. It seemed like Peter was attempting to prevent disturbing a wild animal when he lifted one finger to tell the shooter that he was ready to click the button and make a loud sound; it was like he was trying to keep the gunman from being scared.

What are you going to do now, pal? I'll open the register for you.

The guy told them to "shut the fuck up and get on with it.".

Peter gently raised his index finger and said, "John."

To my surprise, John had moved a few feet closer to the action. Peter ordered him to put his scissors down on the counter, so he did as he was told.

Asked John, "Do you want to die today or something?" the guy with the pistol levelled the weapon towards him.

"Not at all, buddy. "It was only a matter of lowering the blades."

The Irishman stayed in the line of fire.

Peter called out, "Hey, friend." "Keep your head down."

When the assailant re-aimed, he saw Peter‘ chest as a target.

It's time to open the till, Peter said. "And then you're going to walk out of here, right?"

The assailant swallowed once more before pointing his revolver at the cash register. "Get going, you fuckas!"

Kaching.

The cash register's chime served as the man's starting gun. In order to guarantee he was not disturbed, he rushed to the cash drawer and crammed notes into his hoodie pocket.

"Have a little fun with that," John urged.

While continuing to empty the cash register, the guy laughed it off. Peter made a calming gesture to John.

“Hey!” Jim exclaimed. We’ve worked hard for it, jerk.

John was directly in the line of fire as the assailant approached. Incredibly, he said, "Do you think I give a shit?" "Out there, it’s every guy for himself."

"It doesn’t have to be that way," I found myself saying, even though my voice was little and high-pitched. It sounded like a cliche. Having to cope with a melancholy high school student who is utterly out of his depth.

The guy took a few breaths before he glared at me. "Have you heard the latest news?" It’s already that w—, however.

Peter made a lunging attack on the assailant, his hands grabbing for the pistol. Using his free hand, the guy fended Peter away from the pistol. Peter tried to throw himself again, but he slipped and fell to the ground because of the hair on the floor. After the gunman’s pocket was emptied of cash, Peter grabbed his ankle and pulled him to the ground as he tried to pick it up.

The two men had vanished from view when John dashed into the fray, and I heard what sounded like a firecracker or maybe two pieces of wood slamming together right next to my ears. John staggered back, his white t-shirt stained with red wine, and the wine that came out of John’s mouth was thicker, viscous, thicker than water—that what’s slur?

There’s nothing I can do about it. A crack could be heard as Peter fought the man behind the counter, but otherwise there was silence. John was bleeding and then fell to his knees, his eyes wide and confused. He pleaded with me silently, and I wanted to apologise like it was my fault. But his eyes turned grey and there was no more sound.

A familiar raspy puffing was drowned out by Peter wrestling the gunman and the scurrying of their feet into the thick hair.

As soon as he stood up, he shoved the money inside his sweatshirt and wiped the perspiration from his face with the back of his hand.

It was all Peter's fault, he pointed the rifle towards Peter's corpse and yelled at him. As if Peter standing up for him and his barbershop was some kind of personal affront, he seemed enraged. Then there's John," he said, pointing at him. "I mean, he leaped on me." "What am I meant to do now?" It seemed as if the guy had been startled, and his ghostly pallor had changed to a greyish green colour. He drew in a few quick breaths.

He broke down and sobbed.

When I saw him, he looked so sad and retched with snot running from his nose, I felt sorry for him. A stream of cash poured out of his hoodie's zippered pocket. As useless as dry leaves, he decided not to gather them this time.

Pal, what's your name? I stated my opinion. In order to avoid being shot, I did not want to be his buddy.

"What?" he inquired, perplexed.

"I'll call you by your given name. "Who are you?"

Finally, "Jeff" came out of his mouth after the man seemed to forget for a second.

"Okay, Jeff," I responded despite the fact that it sounded like a fictitious name. "We're leaving right now."

Jeff paused before replying. It was a simple, "Yeah, alright" on his part.

He was astonished when I arose from my chair and the shop's dynamic suddenly changed. Once again, I felt the jolt of his rifle in my temples.

"I beg of you, gentlemen. Jeff. My two little children are eagerly awaiting my arrival at home."

"What? There there no children in your family?"

Thank you, Jeff. I really appreciate it. So, why don't we put our attention on our children? Tonight, they'll be eager to see us, right? It's time for bedtime tales.

When Jeff saw my shoulder, the rifle aimed above his head. "Drop your w-" was yelled by a voice behind me before Jeff's revolver hushed it. First, Jeff jerked his left shoulder back and then his right; it seemed to be like he was dancing in a film clip, but it was really him jerking his shoulders back in convulsions. His body was found on the barbershop floor after he flung his head back and died.

Jeff's body was thrown on its stomach and shackled by two blue blurs, who murmured commands into their radios.

Another individual led me back to the red leather chair at some time.. My feet had lost their weight, noises were becoming muffled under the ringing, and strange aromas filled my nostrils, giving me the impression that I was in a dream.

I was being interrogated by a woman in a police outfit, but all I could see was my own reflection.

Scattered with dark crimson staining, my hair was cut into a clean carpet of silver fluff while the other half was a rough imitation of my old hairdo. According to my official testimony, I asked the police woman if she could complete my haircut, but I have no recall of saying so.

Since the shooting at Peter's Cuts, I haven't gotten my hair cut. Because of the lockdown and the severe financial condition, it's safe to say. Peter and John would be proud of the way my hair has grown out. Despite the fact that it has grown in length, one side is nice and orderly, while the other is wild and vulnerable to even the smallest wind.

But I'm unable to bring myself to shave it off. It would be an even bigger betrayal to eradicate the traces of Peter and his cutters.

The man is Peter Lopez. The virus's first victim; the last guy to cut my hair.

CHAPTER FIVE

# Ringer of death

In the early morning hours of Isan Thailand, it was just after 2 a.m. Early risers, particularly farmers, were well-known in this region of Thailand, especially those who had the additional burden of relying on their own resources to live. However, even Neung fell asleep at these times. An continuous pinging had woken him from a deep and undisturbed sleep in the middle of the night.

Evening prayers, soaking rice in water for tomorrow's Khao Tom breakfast, and shutting all the windows were all part of his nighttime routines as a good Thai, and he was ready for a good night's sleep. As luck would have it, it was the full moon of Ok Phansa in late October, which meant that the temperature wasn't as sweltering as it typically would have been.

That implies Neung and his family were low-income sharecroppers on a medium-sized rice paddy in their village; they couldn't even afford what most Westerners would consider luxuries. As a result, he slept on a narrow mat and wore just a modest cloth covering as his bed linens. Years of sleeping on wooden floors and meditating in temples had rendered him resistant to the aches and pains that come with ritual practise, which is fortunate for him. A good hardwood teak floor did wonders for the back after spending days at a time stooped over in shin-deep water during rice harvesting season. Even yet, he couldn't help but appreciate the sleep he was given.

It was now hard to ignore the systematic shouting. Washing his face fast, he swiftly wiped the sleep out of his eyes. His sole light source at night was a low-burning kerosene lamp. Bodies jostling in the stilt clay and straw huts were audible to him. While wild soi-dogs howled in the distance, chickens moved nervously cooing. The neighbours must have woken up as well, since the squeaks and stomps were heard across the street. I'd say this warranted additional study.

Even though Neung and his fellow villagers resisted the urge to leave the hamlet in the middle of the night, they were captivated by the music and could no longer ignore it. On this full moon, Thailand's mysterious environment was bathed in an auspicious sense of dread, as the moon's low position in the sky produced an ominous aura. This belief was based on the belief that the dead may rejoin with the living on certain specific days, much like Celt and Pagan celebrations of All Hallow's Eve and Samhain, All Saint's Day and Dia De Los Muertos, among others. The Thai Wive's Club, an unofficial group of women in the area, was abuzz with rumours about the extraordinary events of the night, which fueled the local belief in superstition.

To show respect for those who persevered despite the noise, Thailand's idea of "Kreng Jai" meant that no one would be starting their loud 110cc motorcycles. Neung's group of exhausted neighbours had no choice but to walk to the source of the pinging since no one else in the village possessed a car. Aside from a few feeble flashlights and a few bulbs, there was not enough light to illuminate the path in front of them. It was fortunate for Neung that he had spent his whole life on these pathways and rice field embankments, so he could virtually navigate them blindfolded. Even while he seemed to be a confident leader, the truth was that he was equally terrified of the wandering dead and a cobra, both of which are frequent in this area.

Villagers went through an overgrown reeds and pathways labyrinth, all agreeing that the noise, whatever it was, looked to be emanating from the town's only temple as they passed by it. This was the heart of the community. As a matter of fact, it was the hallowed temple grounds and its ornate architecture that differentiated one community from another. However, it was also a location where the deceased may be entombed and laid to rest in peace. Moreover, it was the only portion of town that was completely isolated from the rest of the world, a phrase that is used loosely in this rural, semi-structured region. Monks also spent many hours there meditating, conversing with their deceased ancestors, and even attempting to attain enlightenment, which was exceedingly improbable in the big scheme of cosmic time.

When the shadows of palm trees or grazing water buffalo appeared in the distance, they seemed to take on the appearance of demonic apparitions or wandering spirits. The residents' already frazzled nerves weren't helped by the noise. Thais have a historical tradition of giving spectral forms to sinners who committed their crimes while remaining on this planet. There were towering ones, flying ones, and luminous ones among the crowd. " Inquisitive ones with small stitched lips and those with entrails hanging out. There were both sea and forest ghosts. Ghosts that don't have heads and those that have arms that can extend. A sin or wicked thinking has been attached to almost every demon or spirit incarnation or human disease or disfigurement.

In Thailand, life was like a morality play at times. In an effort to keep children and adults from succumbing to the temptations of sin, the society has accepted most extraterrestrial appearances. The issue is that it has been pushed to the limit. Nearly eighty percent of those polled claimed to have had some kind of encounter with a ghost or paranormal activity, and even more said they believed in the reality of such things. There were many examples of it in everything from television to movies and music. This was a place where living with ghosts, most of whom were trying to terrify you into doing the right thing, was commonplace and accepted. They also had a strong belief in rebirth. As a haunting ghost, you would have many chances to atone for your transgressions before being reincarnated as a human again, which was considered the peak of human life.

Folklore about ghosts was passed down from generation to generation along this path. During one of the many nights of Khun Lek's great aunt's wake, she was chased by a ghost that was dragging its own coffin by the chains as she made her way home. However, there were also stories of those who had been awakened from their restless sleep by the revelry of numerous full moon ravers on the beaches that had been ravaged by the huge tsunami, only to discover that no one was there. As to an additional legend, locals would be forced to accommodate the ghostly figures' request for a midnight movie showing deep in the bush by the villages, only to discover that no one had shown up the next morning.

Neung and his neighbours, on the other hand, had little interest in such matters. They were only trying to figure out where the noise was coming from at this point. Anyone within a five-kilometer radius of the culprit had been awakened by the person who had not been practising "kreng jai." In this socially conscious Southeast Asian society, selfishness considered the worst of all sins. As soon as they came home and realised what had happened, Neung couldn't help but think about the surge of local customers at the farmers market that would occur as soon as they woke up and got ready. In other words, you won't be able to get any shuteye tonight. In his position, he could not afford to miss a day's work owing to a night of sleep deprivation, even if the Hindenburg itself had crashed on his shack.

Despite the throng's bad energy and its appearance as a pitchfork-wielding crowd, they suddenly became serene as they passed through the temple gates under the watchful eye of Naga, its guardian serpent. At this point, they were not outraged but rather awestruck by what they had just seen.

The temple's enormous brass bell was the source of the noise they had been hearing from the beginning. An activity that is traditionally reserved for rare occasions and undertaken by professed monks of the cloth, rather than ordinary citizens. When the full harvest moon was casting a spell over the witching hours, these things never happened.

In their minds, Neung and his company anticipated to witness a trance-induced monk who was meditating and communicating with spirits in an other reality that none of them had the mental capacity to observe. But as they viewed it, it had no place on a temple's sacred grounds.

It was a womanly figure on an elevated platform, dressed only in a gory nightgown and exhibiting her female form, which was banned in the temple. Her bleeding torso and breasts were covered in a blanket of tears. Heavily weighted mallet she had been using to hammer out her cries for assistance on the brass "rakhang" had quadrupled the size of her emaciated hands. "Why?" she repeatedly muttered as her blue-black veins swelled beyond all recognition. As a result, her face seemed hollowed and depleted.

A lady collapsed in the throng after uttering the word "Noi" simply once. Noi had been identified by the people as Neung's bride; his adored. Although her corpse had never been located, some believe she was killed for blood money some 50 years earlier after she was brutally abused until she was finally tortured and then slain.

9 798887 493831

Printed by Libri Plureos GmbH in Hamburg,
Germany